FUELED FOR ADVENTURE

D0168554

Golden® First Chapters

A Golden Book • New York

Materials and characters from the movie *Cars 2*. Copyright © 2011 Disney/Pixar.
Disney/Pixar elements © Disney/Pixar, not including underlying vehicles owned by third
parties; and, if applicable: Pacer and Gremlin are trademarks of Chrysler LLC; Jeep®
and the Jeep® grille design are registered trademarks of Chrysler LLC; Porsche is a
trademark of Porsche; Sarge's rank insignia design used with the approval of the U.S.
Army; Volkswagen trademarks, design patents and copyrights are used with the approval
of the owner, Volkswagen AG; Bentley is a trademark of Bentley Motors Limited; FIAT is
a trademark of FIAT S.p.A.; Corvette and Chevrolet Impala are trademarks of General
Motors. All rights reserved. Published in the United States by Golden Books, an imprint
of Random House Children's Books, a division of Random House, Inc., 1745 Broadway,
New York, NY 10019, and in Canada by Random House of Canada Limited, Toronto,
in conjunction with Disney Enterprises, Inc. Golden Books, A Golden Book, and the G
colophon are registered trademarks of Random House, Inc. Golden First Chapters is a
trademark of Random House, Inc.

ISBN: 978-0-7364-2820-0
GLB ISBN: 978-0-7364-8102-1

www.randomhouse.com/kids
Printed in the United States of America
10 9 8 7 6 5 4 3 2

Random House Children's Books supports the First Amendment and celebrates the
right to read.

FUELED FOR ADVENTURE

Adapted by Christine Peymani
and Adam B. Murr

Illustrated by Carson Van Osten

My name is McMissile—Finn McMissile. Some cars call me a spy, but I prefer "secret agent." My job is to bring villains to justice. If I do my job right, most cars will never know I exist.

My mission began when Special Agent Leland Turbo sent me a message—from the middle of the ocean!

"I've stumbled onto something massive," Turbo whispered urgently. I could barely see him on the video feed. The signal kept breaking up. "Need to get my data in . . . lives will be lost!" He never finished the message. "They've found me!" was the last thing I heard.

Turbo needed help, and headquarters needed

his data. There was no time to lose. I set out to find him.

Within hours, I had hitched a ride on a small crab boat. We were heading out to sea, to Turbo's last location. The night was dark. The waves tossed us up and down. Suddenly, a bright spotlight shone on us.

"What are you doing out here?" a huge speedboat boomed. I figured we were in the right place. Why else would a security boat be out here?

"What's it look like? Crabbing!" my feisty little crab boat snapped in reply.

While the speedboat was distracted, I sneaked onto his hull. Soon, we were racing across the water. It wasn't long before I saw a group of massive oil derricks. They were tall structures, pumping oil from the ocean floor. The speedboat pulled up to one. I used my built-in climbing cables to pull myself up the side of the derrick.

I shut off my engine and rolled into the

shadows. A group of ugly little vehicles huddled on the deck below. They were all Gremlins and Pacers.

But why were they here? Who were they working for?

Using my cables, I slid into position high above the scene. A secret camera popped out of my headlight. I began snapping photos. One close-up showed a large video camera. There were three big letters on its side: WGP.

Suddenly, there was a murmur in the crowd below. Someone important had arrived.

"Out of the way!" a car shouted in a German accent. It was Professor Z, a well-known scientist—and criminal. I knew he was the car in charge.

Just then, I noticed Turbo next to Professor Z. The poor fellow had been crushed into a lump of metal!

As I stared in horror, a light flared at the top of the rig. My shadow fell across the deck. Professor Z looked up.

"It's Finn McMissile!" he shouted.

The Gremlins and Pacers swarmed toward me. Quickly, I cut myself loose from my cables. I swung down and landed on the deck. Then I sped up a nearby ramp. The bad guys were close on my fender, so I sprayed oil behind me. That sent a few of them sliding off the side of the derrick.

When I reached the top of the ramp, there was nowhere to go. So I leaped off the side and plunged straight into the deep water below.

Suddenly, a crew of heavily armed boats began firing missiles at me. There were explosions all around. For a moment, I didn't think I'd be able to escape. As a last resort, I dived deep underwater and switched to submarine mode. The missile firing stopped.

Good, I thought. Professor Z and his crew thought I was dead. There is no better cover for a secret agent.

CHAPTER 2

While I was on the oil derrick, key events were unfolding in a little American town called Radiator Springs. These events would change the course of my entire mission.

It all began with a rusty old tow truck named Mater. He was waiting for his best friend, Lightning McQueen, to return home. The famous American race car had just won the Hudson Hornet Memorial Piston Cup.

"Oh, boy! Oh, boy!" Mater said. He was so excited. He had made a "Welcome Home" sign for Lightning out of a pile of tires, an old battery, and some lights. It was alarming what that chap could create out of simple junk.

Mater waited and waited for Lightning to

arrive. In fact, he waited so long that he fell asleep! When Lightning finally rolled into town, Mater was snoring.

Lightning and his Radiator Springs friends gathered around Mater. Finally, someone blew his horn. The tow truck jumped up in surprise. He was so startled that he shot backward, swerved all the way through town, and fell over a cliff.

Everyone raced to see if Mater was all right. But he came back up over the dusty cliff smiling.

"Wow, you just got yourself a nasty dent there, Mater," said Lightning.

Oddly, Mater didn't seem to mind. To him, a dent was a sign of friendship.

Later that evening, Lightning went out for a quiet dinner with his girlfriend, Sally. But the entire town joined them to celebrate Lightning's victory. Mater was there, too.

Just then, Sir Miles Axlerod came on the restaurant's TV screen. He was being interviewed on a talk show. Everyone in the restaurant listened closely. Axlerod had made a fortune in the oil industry. But now he was changing his business. He had created a clean, alternative fuel called Allinol. He wanted everyone to use it.

The television reporter explained Axlerod's plan. "To show the world what his new super-fuel can do, he's created a racing competition like no other, inviting the greatest champions from around the globe to battle in the first-ever World Grand Prix!"

There would be three races in three different countries—Japan, Italy, and England. All the race cars would use Allinol. Lightning McQueen was the only champion who was not racing.

Lightning stared at the TV. He had really wanted some time off to be with Sally and all his friends.

But then the Italian racer Francesco Bernoulli appeared on the TV screen.

"Lightning McQueen would not have a chance against Francesco!" he boasted.

Mater was so angry, he ran straight to the telephone and called in to the show!

"That Italian fella on there can't talk that way about Lightning McQueen," Mater declared. "Lightning could drive circles around you!"

Francesco smiled. "Driving in circles is all he can do, no?" Then he turned to the interviewer. "Can we move on? Francesco needs a caller who can provide a little more intellectual stimulation. Like a dump truck."

That did it. In moments, Lightning was on the phone, too. "I don't appreciate my best friend being insulted!" he declared.

The argument grew from there. Finally, Lightning decided to accept Francesco's challenge. To teach Francesco a lesson, he would race in the World Grand Prix after all. And he would take his friends—including Mater, Sarge, Fillmore, Luigi, and Guido.

Shortly after that, my path would cross Lightning and Mater's in a most unusual way.

CHAPTER 3

When I arrived at Sir Miles Axlerod's World Grand Prix party in Tokyo, it was filled with famous race cars and their teams. They were a smart and classy group.

I was not there for the party, however. I was trying to find a link between the World Grand Prix and the video camera I had seen on the derrick. The letters on the camera matched the World Grand Prix logo.

"Eeee-yah!" someone screamed. From my spot on the balcony, I noticed a rusty tow truck splashing in a water fountain below. It was that chap Mater.

A few moments later, the tow truck had a small oil spill—right in front of Axlerod. "But I

never leak oil!" said the embarrassed truck.

I focused on the cameras that were recording the party. Each one had the letters WGP on its side, just like the one on the derrick. My computer scanned them all. None matched Professor Z's.

As I thought this over, a sleek young sports car parked beside me. "A Volkswagen Karmann Ghia has no radiator," she whispered.

I had never seen her before, but she knew the agency code.

"That's because it's air-cooled," I replied, also in code.

"I'm Agent Shiftwell, Holley Shiftwell," she said. "I have a message from London."

We rolled into the elevator to talk in private.

Agent Shiftwell told me that headquarters had gone over my photos from the derrick. But the camera did not appear to be special. "They said perhaps if you could get *closer* pictures next time?" she told me.

I frowned. "A good spy gets what he can, then gets out before he's killed," I said.

Agent Shiftwell continued. Fortunately, an American agent had gone undercover at the oil platform. Somehow he had gotten a photo of the car in charge of the entire operation. "He's here tonight to pass the photo to you," she said.

I nodded, pleased. Something big was up. This would help us figure it out.

"One more thing," she added. "The oil field itself? Turns out it's the largest oil reserve in the world."

I realized then that this was even bigger than I'd guessed.

Just then, I glanced down at the party and spotted a Pacer and two Gremlins from the oil rig. I couldn't let them see me. They thought I was at the bottom of the ocean, and I wanted to keep it that way.

"Change of plan," I told Holley. "*You're* meeting the American."

As she went downstairs, the American agent turned on his tracking device.

"Move in!" I radioed to Holley.

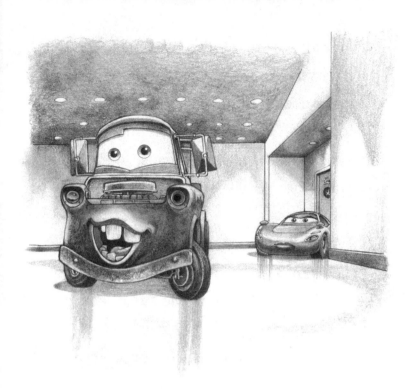

Over the radio, I heard a voice with a thick American accent. "Excuse me, ma'am!"

"This cannot be him," Agent Shiftwell said. She was looking at the rusty old tow truck, Mater!

"A Volkswagen Karmann Ghia has no radiator," Holley said cautiously.

"Of course it doesn't," the tow truck replied. "That's 'cause it's air-cooled!"

Naturally, both Holley and I thought that Mater *was* the American agent. He had answered in agency code, after all.

However, he didn't give us the photo. We thought he was nervous because our enemies were nearby. Holley suggested meeting at a later time.

"When can I see you again?" she asked.

They agreed to meet at the race the next day. The World Grand Prix would be a good cover for us.

Little did I know that our enemy had kidnapped the real American agent. Just before the agent was taken, he had stuck the recording device with his top-secret information on Mater. The tow truck had no idea.

CHAPTER 4

The first race began the next evening. Agent Shiftwell and I were ready. From a nearby skyscraper, we could see everything. There were crowds of fans and armies of workers. The racers were warming up.

I focused on the WGP cameras near the racetrack. I had to find that camera from the oil derrick.

Meanwhile, Holley used a telescopic lens to search for Mater.

She found him in a most unusual spot. "Why's he in the pits?" she asked. Mater was talking to the pit crew for Team Lightning McQueen! I focused my lens on him.

"It's his cover," I answered. "One of the best

I've seen, too. Look at the detail on his rust. Must have cost a fortune." We still had no idea that Mater was not a real agent.

Holley and I waited for Mater to contact us.

"Hold on," Holley said suddenly. She had spotted a suspicious car in the crowd. "The Pacer from the party last night!" She looked at the photos I had taken at the oil derrick. "His VIN numbers match," she said.

This Pacer had been at the oil derrick, at the party . . . and he was here as well.

Holley scanned the crowd. Suddenly, she saw dozens of Gremlins and Pacers. They were all headed toward Mater! They clearly thought he was the American agent, too. And they were closing in!

I rushed away from our lookout. Agent Shiftwell stayed behind to contact Mater.

"Get him out of the pits!" I said through the radio. "Now!"

As I sped toward the pit area, the crowd gasped. A race car had spun out and crashed.

That gave me a chance to slip unnoticed into the pit area for Team Lightning McQueen.

Mater disappeared. I hoped I wasn't too late.

Suddenly, the doors to the pit area flew open. The Pacer from the derrick stared at me!

"Finn McMissile!" he exclaimed. "But you're dead!"

Blast it all! I thought. Quickly, I sprayed him in the eyes with a fire extinguisher and sped off.

Holley radioed that Mater was in the back alley. Dozens of Professor Z's Gremlins and Pacers were nearby.

"Keep him moving," I told Holley. "I'm on my way."

I drove fast, but Professor Z's cars were soon on my fender.

I had to give the American time to get away. I activated my defenses. Immediately, protective armor wrapped around my tires. *"Hee-YA!"* I yelled. The fight was on!

One by one, the cars attacked. But karate is one of my best skills. I threw one thug onto a

giant neon sign. I sent the others flying through the air.

To my surprise, Mater stayed and watched. "Wow, a live karate demonstration!" I heard him say. "Give 'em a right! Now a left! Left! Left-right!"

I defeated the last of Professor Z's little cars. Then I followed Mater back to the race pits. I hoped he would give me that secret device.

Instead, I found him with Lightning McQueen. They were arguing.

"I lost the race because of you!" Lightning shouted. He was upset that Mater had left the pits.

"I'm sorry," said Mater. He looked upset, too. I thought he was playing along very well. "I didn't mean to—"

"I don't want your help!" yelled Lightning. He zoomed away. I heard Mater mutter something about the airport.

I was sure he had staged the fight as an excuse to leave. I told Agent Shiftwell to prepare for a meeting at the airport.

CHAPTER 5

At the Tokyo airport, I disguised myself as a security officer. "Come with me, please," I said to Mater.

"But I'm gonna miss my plane!" Mater protested.

I led him around the corner and dropped my disguise. "Finn McMissile. British intelligence," I said.

"Tow Mater. Average intelligence," he replied.

I was impressed by how well Mater stuck to his cover as an ordinary tow truck. If only I had known that it wasn't a cover at all!

Suddenly, I spotted the troublesome Pacer and Gremlin. They were about to close in.

Mater and I were in a waiting area next to the runway. There was no clear exit. I used a laser to cut through the glass of a nearby window. Then I hooked onto Mater's tow line and revved my engine. I leaped through the glass window— and pulled Mater right behind me. We landed— *bang!*—on the runway below.

Skidding, I whipped Mater in front of me. "Drive forward!" I yelled.

While I was being towed, I could see our enemies head-on as they gave chase.

But just then, my good friend Siddeley, a British spy jet, flew down and opened his ramp for us. We could see Agent Shiftwell inside.

"Come on!" Holley shouted. "Get in here!"

I hit my brakes and skidded again. Mater spun behind me this time. With a last burst of energy, I pulled us both onto the ramp. The jet soared upward just in time.

CHAPTER 6

Once we were in the air, Holley turned to Mater. It was time to collect his secret data. She took out a robotic arm. Then she yanked the recording device from beneath him and loaded it into our computer.

"Time to see who's behind all this," Holley said.

A dark image formed in front of us. It showed a complicated mix of metallic parts. We had no idea what it was.

"That's one of the worst engines ever made," Mater said. "It's an old aluminum Leyland V8 with Whitworth bolts." He explained that the Whitworth bolts were very unusual.

"Whose engine is this, Mater?" asked Holley.

Mater eyed the photo. "It's kinda hard to tell from this picture, ain't it?" he said.

Agent Shiftwell repeated what she'd learned earlier. "A good spy gets what he can, then gets out before he's killed."

"You guys is spies!" Mater exclaimed. I thought he was joking.

Frankly, I wasn't sure what to make of the photo. The engine did not tell me very much about the head of the evil operation.

But Mater explained that the engine was considered a clunker. Except that most of its parts had been replaced by rare, original parts.

I wondered if the parts were a clue.

"I know of a black-market parts dealer in Paris," I said. "He's a treacherous lowlife, but he's the only car in the world who can tell us whose engine this is."

I looked at Mater. "What would you say to forming an informal task force on this one?" I asked. "You obviously have plenty of experience in the field."

"But you know I'm just a tow truck, right?" he asked.

"Right," I replied with a wink. "And I'm in the import-export business."

I called out to Siddeley. It was time to kick into high speed. Next stop: Paris, France!

CHAPTER 7

Paris is a beautiful city. We weren't visiting the nice areas, though. Instead, I led Mater and Agent Shiftwell through back alleys. Graffiti and trash were everywhere.

"Stay close," I warned Holley. "Don't talk to anyone. Don't look at anyone. And absolutely no idling."

"Yes, sir," Agent Shiftwell replied.

We turned the corner. A crowd of broken-down cars filled the street in front of us. Mater looked alarmed.

Luckily, I soon found my informant. Tomber was a three-wheeled car with shifty eyes. He was a crooked car parts dealer. But I was sure he'd know about that strange engine.

When Tomber saw us, he raced away. He wanted me to chase him, of course. He had to make it look like I was his enemy. If anyone saw us speaking in the open, he would lose his business. But once we were alone in an empty garage, Tomber smiled and spoke freely.

Holley showed Tomber the photo of the strange engine.

Tomber whistled. "What a bucket of bolts!" Then he looked closer. "Wait. The *parts*. Original from the manufacturer!" Tomber hadn't seen such rare and expensive parts in years. But he couldn't identify the engine's owner.

"Mater," Holley pleaded. "Is there anything else you can tell us about this engine?"

"Sorry," Mater replied. "I told you everything I know about this Lemon."

We all looked at him curiously. We asked him what a "Lemon" was.

"You know," Mater said. "Cars that don't work right. Lemons are a tow truck's bread and butter. Like those Pacers and Gremlins at the party and race and airport and such? They're Lemons, too."

Mater was right! Lemons were turning up everywhere. Holley projected my photos from the oil derrick. In addition to the Gremlins and Pacers, we spotted Hugos and Trunkovs. They were all Lemons. Even Professor Z was a Lemon.

"This explains it," Tomber said suddenly. "There've been rumors of a secret meeting of these so-called Lemon cars in Porto Corsa in two days."

The second race of the World Grand Prix would be in Porto Corsa, Italy. We didn't think it was a coincidence.

I contacted headquarters and made plans to go to Porto Corsa right away. We had to find out why the Lemon clans were meeting. Then we might learn who was behind this operation— and why.

CHAPTER 8

We rode to Porto Corsa in a private car on a high-speed train. Our car was filled with computer equipment. Holley made good use of it on our ride.

First, she reprogrammed all the traffic lights in Porto Corsa. The lights took photographs of every intersection in the city. Then the computer sent the photos to us.

"Wow!" Mater said to Agent Shiftwell. "Not only is you the prettiest car I ever met, you're the *smartest*, too!"

"Thank you," Holley replied curtly. "I think."

Mater stared at the photographs of Porto Corsa like a new car in a tire shop. He couldn't stop counting all the Lemons that swarmed through the streets of the little Italian city.

"Look at that Hugo there," Mater noted. "He looks perfect, but he's being towed around anyhows."

Mater was right. The car was waxed, polished, and freshly painted. Yet he was unable—or unwilling—to run his engine.

"Hmmm," I muttered. "He must be one of the heads of the Lemon families." Perhaps the Lemonheads didn't have the parts they needed to run anymore. Or they didn't want to over-use what they had. Either way, the Lemonheads needed *tow trucks* to pull them around.

"We've got to infiltrate that meeting," I said. I was sure our mystery enemy would be there. Or that he would at least deliver a message. "It's the only way to find out who's behind this."

But I wasn't sure how we would do it. I glanced at Agent Shiftwell. I could see that she had an idea.

"Hang on," she said to Mater. Then she snapped a photograph of his face.

"Ahh!" Mater shouted in surprise.

In no time, Agent Shiftwell was hard at work on the computer again. By mixing different photos, she placed Mater's face on the Hugo's tow truck. Then she used the image to create an electronic holo-disguise for Mater.

"It's voice-activated," she told Mater.

"What?" Mater asked. I thought he was just playing dumb. "Hey, I thought you were supposed to be making me a disguise."

Agent Shiftwell's work was superb. The

computer responded automatically to his words. "Voice recognized. Disguise program initiated."

A holographic image of the Lemonhead's tow truck was projected onto Mater's body. "Cool!" he cried.

There were a few problems, though. The disguise didn't fit over Mater's dents. Agent Shiftwell needed to fix them.

Mater refused. "Well, then, no, thank you! I don't get those dents buffed, pulled, filled, or painted by nobody. They're way too valuable," he said. "I came by each one of them with my best friend, Lightning McQueen."

Agent Shiftwell and I paused. Secret agents did not have close friendships. But Mater's friendship with Lightning McQueen was beginning to sound real. We probably should have suspected then that Mater wasn't a real spy. But we shrugged it off.

"I'll work around the dent," Holley agreed.

Soon, Mater was ready to sneak into the Lemonheads' meeting.

CHAPTER 9

When we arrived in Porto Corsa, the city was buzzing with excitement about the second race of the World Grand Prix. The Italian fans hoped Francesco would win.

A television announcer talked about the upcoming race. "The big news continues to be Allinol," he said. "Sir Miles Axlerod spoke to the press earlier today to answer questions about its safety." A car had exploded during the first race in Tokyo. It was using Allinol. Axlerod said the fuel was safe. But everyone wondered if that was true.

In fact, Lightning's team was talking to him about Allinol at that very moment. His friend Fillmore, a VW van, was a fuel expert. "If you're worried about your fuel, man, don't be," said Fillmore. "It's perfectly safe."

We drove up the winding roads toward the Lemons' big meeting. The Porto Corsa casino was elegant. It was also full of guards and security cameras. We were sure it was the Lemons' secret meeting spot. I settled across the street at a cafe where I could keep an eye on things. Holley and Mater moved into position.

"I don't know about this," Mater whispered to me over his radio. He was hidden around a corner, waiting while Holley approached one of the tow trucks outside the casino.

"Just apply the same level of dedication you've been using to play the idiot tow truck and you'll be fine," I replied.

Mater paused. "Wait. Did you say 'idiot'? That's how you see me?"

"That's how everyone sees you. Isn't that the idea?" I said. I still didn't realize it wasn't an act. "That's the genius of it. No one realizes they're being fooled because they're too busy

laughing *at* the fool. Brilliant cover, Mater!"

Mater was silent. I didn't realize that I had insulted him.

Suddenly, we saw Holley. She led the Hugo Lemonhead's tow truck around the corner. Then she zapped him unconscious.

It was time for Mater to activate his holo-disguise. In no time, Mater looked just like the Lemonhead's tow truck!

In disguise, Mater came out of his hiding place. He headed toward the Hugo security team. His timing was perfect! The Hugos were watching a limo pull up.

"It's the boss! He's coming!" the Hugos shouted. They bowed as the door opened. A polished old Hugo rolled out. It was Victor. He was the head of the Hugo Lemons.

"Ivan!" he shouted. Mater turned. Victor was staring right at him.

Mater knew what to do. He latched his hook to Victor and towed him into the casino. Mater was on the inside.

CHAPTER 10

Holley watched the front of the casino from around a corner. "Maybe now we'll find out who's behind all this," she radioed to me. My main concern was Mater, however. He was inside the casino with the Lemonheads. "Wow! This place looks like it's made of gold!" he exclaimed into his secret radio.

"That's because it is, Mater. Be careful what you say," Agent Shiftwell radioed in reply.

"So you want me to stop talking to you? Right now?" Mater asked.

Then we heard another voice—it was a Lemon. "You're acting strange today, Ivan," he said.

I froze. I was sure Mater had blown his cover.

"I have no idea what you're talking about," Mater replied.

Finally, the same Lemon spoke again. "Don't mess with Ivan today," he told the other Lemons. "He's in a bad mood." Mater had pulled it off! The Hugos believed he was Ivan.

"He's so blasted *good*!" I told Holley.

Holley watched the display from Mater's camera. Professor Z entered the room. He turned to a wall of video monitors.

Suddenly, all the monitors showed the engine from our mysterious photo, complete with Whitworth bolts! But this time, it was a live image. The engine belonged to the Lemons' leader. He spoke to the crowd while his engine was being worked on. He did not reveal his identity.

"Welcome," he said. The video disguised his voice. "I wish I could be with you on this very special day, but . . . my clutch assembly broke. You know how it is."

The Lemons nodded.

"We're here to celebrate," he continued. "Today, all of your hard work pays off." He paused. "The world turned their back on cars like us. They stopped manufacturing us, stopped making our parts. The only thing they haven't stopped doing is laughing at us!"

The Lemons listened as he listed all the nicknames for defective cars: jalopy, rust bucket, heap, clunker, beater, wreck, and . . . Lemon.

Then his voice grew steely. "But what they consider taunts just gives us strength. Because today, my friends, that all ends."

Every video screen switched to live footage of the WGP race. It was underway just outside.

Suddenly—*BOOM!*

On the screen, one of the racers spun out of control. Smoke poured from her hood.

Inside the casino, the Lemons cheered.

Their leader had *caused* the crash!

CHAPTER 11

Holley and I quickly moved to the side of the casino. We looked down on the racecourse. A plume of smoke was coming from the Brazilian racer's engine.

BOOM! Another racer blew his engine.

Holley looked at her computer. "I'm detecting high levels of electromagnetic radiation," she said. She traced the radiation to a ridge above the course. We looked over and spotted the Gremlin and Pacer we'd seen earlier.

"Finn, it's the camera!" Holley cried.

She was right. The Gremlin and the Pacer had the same camera I had seen at the oil derrick. They were using it to shoot an electromagnetic laser at the racers. The laser

made the Allinol in the racers' engines blow up!

I was sure that Professor Z and the Lemonheads had sent the Gremlin and Pacer to blow up all the World Grand Prix racers. I had to stop them!

I raced toward the opposite ridge. I swerved at top speed around the winding hillside roads. The Gremlin and the Pacer were directly ahead.

I jumped across the ravine to reach them. I wouldn't let another car get hurt on my watch! But suddenly, my body froze in midair.

"What in the world?" I tried to drop to the ground. But it was impossible.

A helicopter carrying a giant magnet hovered above me. My roof was stuck tight, as if it had been glued there. I struggled, but the magnet was too strong.

"We figured you might stop by," said the Pacer with a laugh.

"No!" I shouted. Then the Gremlin gave me an electric shock.

I watched helplessly as the Lemons zapped

another racer, and another. One car rammed into the railing, taking out two more. It was horrible. There was nothing I could do to stop it.

As the helicopter carried me away, I hoped Mater was all right. He was still at the Lemonheads' meeting. Through my radio, I could hear the Lemons' leader talking to the Lemons in the casino. "This was to be alternative fuel's day in the sun," he declared. "But after today, everyone will race back to gasoline. And we, the owners of the world's largest untapped oil reserve in the world, will become the most powerful cars in the world!"

The Lemons shouted, "Long live Lemons!"

Just then, Lightning McQueen and Francesco Bernoulli were fighting to win the race. With a burst of speed, Lightning crossed the finish line first. Neither car knew that the other racers were in trouble.

As the race ended, the Lemons in the casino finally quieted down. Professor Z pointed to the television screens. A reporter was interviewing

Sir Miles Axlerod. "Will you require all the racers to still run on Allinol?"

"I cannot in good conscience risk the lives of any more race cars," Sir Axlerod replied. "The final race will *not* be run on Allinol."

The room erupted in wild cheers. The Lemons' plan to get rid of Allinol was working!

CHAPTER 12

Outside, Agent Shiftwell was worried. She had seen the helicopter take me away. Mater was still in the casino. She warned him to get out of there. But the Lemon thugs surrounded her!

In the casino, everyone was watching the TV monitors. Mater started to back out of the room, but then he noticed what was on the screen. An interviewer was speaking with Lightning McQueen. "They're letting you choose your fuel for the final race," said the interviewer. "Do you know what it's going to be?"

"Allinol," Lightning replied.

"But after today?" said the interviewer.

"My friend Fillmore says the fuel's safe. That's good enough for me," Lightning said.

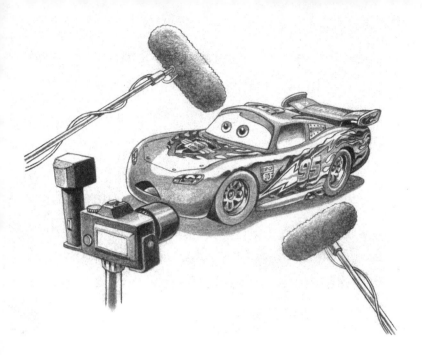

"I didn't stand by a friend of mine recently. I'm not making the same mistake twice."

Lightning was apologizing to Mater on TV!

Inside the casino, Mater could not react without giving himself away. But Professor Z's response was quick. "Allinol must be finished for good," he declared. Professor Z and his mystery Big Boss were determined to make Allinol look bad. They would not let Lightning ruin their plan. "Lightning McQueen must be killed!"

"No!" Mater shouted. He panicked and

knocked into a lightbulb. Electricity zapped through him. His disguise disappeared.

Professor Z recognized Mater at once. "The American spy!"

Agent Shiftwell had given Mater a variety of weapons. He used them to create a distraction. Then Mater escaped onto a balcony. Holley had given him a parachute. He opened it and soared away from the casino. He floated all the way down the hill toward the racetrack. With a few clever moves, Mater landed near the media tent. Lightning McQueen was inside with a crowd of reporters.

"Lemme through!" Mater shouted at the crowd. "I gotta get through to warn Lightning McQueen!"

But when Mater got to the tent, the Lemons were waiting.

That was how Mater, Agent Shiftwell, and I all ended up in London, England.

CHAPTER 13

*B*ong, bong, BONG!

"*Oooh,*" Mater moaned. Agent Shiftwell and I watched as his eyes popped open. We had awoken with the same massive engine ache a few hours earlier. Professor Z and his Lemons had captured each of us separately. Then they had knocked us out and taken us to the same place.

"Holley! Finn!" Mater cried. "What—?"

Mater soon figured out where we were. The giant rotating gears, the loud ticking—we were inside the largest clock in London: Big Bentley. We were tied to the clock's moving gears.

Mater started to struggle. Then the minute hand moved. We all shifted sideways. As the hands moved, we would be pulled slowly into

the gears . . . and crushed into scrap metal.

The last race of the World Grand Prix would soon be speeding by outside. But we might not live to see it.

"This is all my fault," Mater said softly.

"Don't be a fool," I said. After all, risk is part of the game for a secret agent.

"But I am," Mater replied. "You said so."

"When did I—?" I stopped short. I thought back to Porto Corsa. I had told Mater that he played the part of a dimwit brilliantly. "I was complimenting you on what a good spy—"

"I'm not a spy!" Mater interrupted. "I've been trying to tell you that this whole time. I really am just a tow truck!"

"Finn, he's not joking." Agent Shiftwell's voice echoed throughout the clock.

Suddenly, it all made sense. Mater had played dumb so well. He never dropped the act. He was so loyal to Lightning McQueen. I realized that he *was* telling the truth. He wasn't a spy. How could I have been so wrong?

"You were right, Finn. I'm a fool," Mater continued. "And what's happened to Lightning is because I'm such a big one. This is all my fault."

I wanted to correct Mater. He was no fool. He had helped us. We never would have discovered the Allinol plot without him.

But before I could say anything, the Gremlin and the Pacer approached. They had that blasted camera with the laser. They planned to use it right in front of us, as the race cars sped by.

The Gremlin grinned at Mater. "Professor Z wanted you to have a front-row seat for the death of Lightning McQueen."

"He's still alive?" Mater asked hopefully.

"Not for long," the Gremlin and the Pacer sneered. From their perch inside the giant clock tower, the Gremlin and the Pacer had a wide view of the racecourse. The racers would soon drive down the street below us.

The clock ticked.

"There he is," the Gremlin announced. Mater tried to free himself. He cringed as the Lemons aimed the deadly camera laser at Lightning.

Then they fired—but Lightning McQueen sped by unharmed!

We heard the angry voice of Professor Z over a static-filled radio transmission. "What happened?" he yelled.

"I—I don't know," the Gremlin answered. The camera had malfunctioned.

It was time for their "backup plan."

"Backup plan?" Mater asked desperately.

"Yeah," the Gremlin replied. "We snuck a bomb into Lightning McQueen's pit." He grinned as he and the Pacer left.

"Dadgum!" shouted Mater. Then, by golly, he figured out how to use his weapons to free himself. He used his hook to swing to safety.

Then he turned to help us.

"There's no time! It's up to you!" I shouted. "Just go to the pits and get everyone out. You can do that, Mater. Lightning McQueen needs your help!"

CHAPTER 14

Agent Shiftwell used brilliant tactics to free us both. She hit the clock's gearbox with her electroshockers. The shock reversed the clock's gears. As the clock hands moved backward, we were cut free.

But as we headed out, we spotted an air filter on the floor.

"Isn't that Mater's?" Holley asked.

"I knew his escape was too easy!" I could feel my temperature gauge rising. Professor Z and his Lemons had removed Mater's air filter—and replaced it with the bomb! They had known that Mater would rush to Lightning's pit if he thought his friend was in trouble.

Agent Shiftwell and I headed to the pit for

Lightning McQueen. When we arrived, the World Grand Prix racers were still speeding around the course. We swerved through the crowds.

"What are you guys doing here?" I heard Mater shout over the radio. But he wasn't talking to us. He had found all his friends from Radiator Springs in Lightning McQueen's pit.

"We're here because of you, Mater," Sally said. Mater's friends had not heard from him since he had disappeared from the airport, so they had come to London to find him.

"There's a bomb in here!" Mater shouted to his friends. "You all gotta get out now!"

"Mater!" I shouted into the radio.

"Finn!" he exclaimed. "You're okay!" The chap seemed genuinely delighted.

"The bomb is on you!" I told him. "They knew you'd try to help Lightning, so they planted it in your air filter when we were knocked out."

Just then, Lightning McQueen finished a lap and entered his pit. He rushed to greet the tow truck.

Mater moved backward. "Stay away from me!" he shouted as he sped off. Lightning chased him. They drove right into the middle of the racecourse.

"Stay back!" Mater warned his friend again. "If you get close to me, you'll get hurt real bad!"

"I know." Lightning was practically begging Mater to stop and talk. "I made you feel that way before. But none of that matters because we're best friends." Lightning McQueen was giving up his chance to win the race. He wanted to repair his friendship with Mater that badly!

Mater had no choice. Just as Lightning stretched out to grab Mater's hook, *KA-FOOM!* Mater fired up his rockets and blasted away—with Lightning clinging on behind.

Mater and Lightning zoomed away from the racecourse.

Holley and I both took to the streets. Mater needed help!

CHAPTER 15

While Holley raced after Mater, I searched for Professor Z. I found the nasty chap down at the docks, near the River Thames. He was heading for a combat ship that was waiting to help him.

I had just moments to act. Speeding up, I shot my cables at the Professor. They wrapped around his bumper. "Do you really think I'm going to let you float away, Professor?" I asked.

But I couldn't reel him in. Something was pulling him in the opposite direction. I saw that the ship had a giant magnet, which was steadily pulling Professor Z to safety.

The magnet was pulling me in, too. It even pulled my bullets . . . which gave me an idea. I tossed my grenades, rockets, and bombs at the magnet. Suddenly, the whole thing exploded!

Meanwhile, Holley revealed that her own spy equipment included wings! She used her flying gear to soar over the streets of London. She spotted Lemons closing in on Mater and Lightning. She landed swiftly and spun around. A few Lemons were racing toward Mater. Holley knocked them aside.

"We've got to get that bomb off you!" she shouted to Mater.

"Bomb?" Lightning McQueen was shocked. He didn't know anything about the Allinol plot—or about Mater's work as a secret agent.

"Yeah," Mater explained. "They strapped it to me to kill you as a backup plan."

Mater finally understood what was going on— it was as clear as a freshly washed windshield.

That's when I joined the group. Professor Z was with me, tied up as my prisoner. He couldn't escape, but he still had plenty to say.

"You!" Professor Z shouted at Lightning. "Why didn't my death ray kill you?"

It turned out that Lightning had not used Allinol fuel during the race. His friends Fillmore and Sarge had filled the racer's tank with Fillmore's special fuel. It didn't react to the electromagnetic laser like Allinol, so the deadly laser beam had not worked on him.

But we didn't have time to discuss these matters. That bomb was ticking away, and it was stuck on Mater.

"Turn off the bomb!" I ordered Professor Z.

Professor Z sneered. "Are you all so dimwitted?" he asked. "It's voice-activated!"

Mater used his voice. "Deactivate!"

Nothing happened for a moment. Then the timer on the bomb began ticking faster. Now we had just *four minutes* until it exploded!

"It can only be disarmed by the one who activated it," Professor Z declared. "And I am not the one who activated it."

Holley zapped Professor Z unconscious. We had to find the mastermind behind the plot— and fast. But first we had another problem. We

were surrounded by an army of Lemons!

Holley and I flew into action. We used our Academy defense training to fight the Lemons.

Fortunately, we were not battling alone. The cars from Radiator Springs had come to help. Guido, a tiny tire expert, pulled the tires off the Lemons. One car sprayed paint to blind the enemy. A fire truck blasted the Lemons with water. Sarge, a former army car, used remarkable combat tactics.

While everyone else fought, Guido rushed to Mater. The brave little forklift tried to undo the bomb. But he couldn't detach it from Mater.

"None of his wrenches fit the bolts!" someone cried.

Mater looked at the bolts holding the bomb in his engine. Then his eyes lit up.

"I get it! I get it!" he shouted.

Within moments, he hooked onto Lightning. Then Mater activated his parachute and flew skyward.

CHAPTER 16

Holley and I followed Mater and Lightning as fast as we could. They landed at Buckingham Palace, the end of the racecourse. Sir Miles Axlerod was there with the Queen. The palace security team saw the bomb and immediately surrounded Mater.

"Bomb!" they shouted.

I rushed over to Mater. "Mater! I don't know what you're doing, but stand down now!" I had to protect the Queen. I am a British secret agent, after all.

"It's him!" Mater blurted. We all turned and saw Axlerod.

"What?" Axlerod exclaimed.

"I figured it out when I realized y'all attached

this ticking time bomb with Whitworth bolts," Mater said. Mater had noticed Whitworth bolts in the engine that was in the American agent's photo. He had seen them again in the live video feed of the Lemonheads' leader. He knew that the bolts were British. And he was sure they had a British source: Axlerod.

Mater also remembered his little oil spill at the Tokyo party. He had been talking to Axlerod when it happened. But Mater never leaked oil. Leaks were for Lemons. There was only one other car that could have leaked.

"It was *you* leaking oil at the party in Japan," Mater told Axlerod. "You just blamed it on me!"

Mater was sure Axlerod was a Lemon—and the mysterious leader behind the Allinol plot! Holley and I wanted to believe him. But it didn't make sense.

"Axlerod created the race, Mater. Why would he want to hurt anyone?" Holley asked.

"To make Allinol look bad so everyone would go back to oil," Mater answered. "He

said it himself with his disguised voice!"

"You're nuts, you are!" Axlerod cried. "You keep away with that bomb!"

The Queen's guards tried to hustle her away to safety. But she wanted to hear the discussion.

"But Axlerod *created* Allinol," I pointed out. We didn't have any time to waste. That bomb was still ticking!

"Yeah, but what if he found that huge oil field just as the world was trying to find something else?" Mater asked. "What if he came up with Allinol just to make alternative fuel look bad?"

Mater believed that Axlerod owned all those oil derricks. When the world started to turn away from oil, Axlerod had come up with a plan. He would make alternative fuels like Allinol look dangerous. Then, Mater explained, cars everywhere would turn back to old-fashioned fuel. Since Axlerod owned the biggest oil field on the planet, he and his fellow Lemons would become the most powerful cars in the world.

Meanwhile, the bomb was still ticking! With

seconds to go, Mater moved closer to Axlerod. Axlerod shifted nervously. He looked very scared. Suddenly—

"Deactivate!" Axlerod screamed. The bomb froze—one second before it was due to explode.

Mater was right! Axlerod's voice had deactivated the bomb. Mater had proved that Sir Miles Axlerod was behind the whole plot.

Mater used his hook to open Axlerod's hood. Inside was a dirty engine. It dripped oil from all sides. Holley projected the photo we'd received from the American agent. Everyone could see that Axlerod's engine was a perfect match. Axlerod was indeed the mastermind.

The palace guards dragged Axlerod away.

Lightning turned to Mater. "It's official," he said with a smile. "You're coming to all my races from now on."

CHAPTER 17

In all my years of service, I have never met a secret agent as brilliant as Mater. He saved the Queen. He saved the international racers. He saved his best friend, Lightning McQueen. By jove, he saved the entire world from the evil plotting of Miles Axlerod.

It was no wonder that the Queen knighted him. When the ceremonies were over, Mater flew home to Radiator Springs. His friends could not have been prouder.

As for Holley and me? We became official partners. We even flew to Radiator Springs to ask Mater to join our team.

When we arrived, many of the international racers were in town for one final race.

"Oh, man! You guys are gonna have a great time!" Mater said excitedly. Then he glanced at a dent on Holley's side. She had gotten it in the street brawl in London while trying to save Mater.

Mater seemed concerned. "You still got that dent," he told her. "Don't worry. My buddy Ramone can get that fixed up for you in no time."

But Agent Shiftwell had learned from Mater that a dent can be a mark of friendship. "Oh, no," she said. She was smiling. "I'm keeping that dent. It's valuable."

There was no doubt about it. Mater had taught us a lot about friendship—and dents. Holley would keep her dent as a reminder of her friendship with Mater.

The race began. Holley and I watched—until we got an urgent call from headquarters.

"Finn, it's time," Holley said.

"You're leaving already?" Mater asked. The chap looked genuinely disappointed.

That's when I asked him to become a secret

agent. "Her Majesty asked for you personally, Mater," I said.

Mater frowned. He didn't want to hurt our feelings. "But I told you guys before. I ain't a spy," he said.

Agent Shiftwell and I had known that Mater would refuse the job. It was too bad for us. But I was proud of him. He knew who he was and what was important to him.

Still, Holley and I had a job to do. As we turned to leave, I looked at Mater. "Spy or not," I said, "you're still the smartest, most honest chap we've ever met."

Till the end of my days, I will never forget the big grin that spread across Mater's face. As Agent Shiftwell and I jetted away, we smiled, too. Mater was a truck of many talents. But his most important one was his ability to be a good friend. Whether he spent the rest of his days in Radiator Springs or ventured into the spy world again, he would always have friends who understood his true value—dents and all.